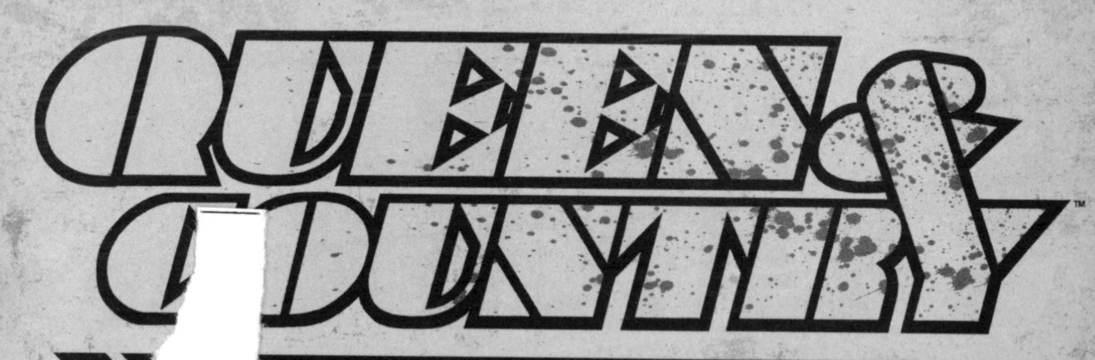

OPERATION: BLACKWALL

Report of Proceedings

- 2 JUN
30
10

OPERATION: BLACKWALL

Report of Proceedings

compiled by **GREG RUCKA**

illustrated by **J. ALEXANDER**

lettering by

JOHN DRANSKI

introduction by

JOHN ROGERS

book design by

KEITH WOOD

collection edited by

JAMES LUCAS JONES

original series edited by

JAMIE S. RICH &
JAMES LUCAS JONES

Published by Oni Press, Inc.
JOE NOZEMACK, publisher
JAMES LUCAS JONES, editor in chief
RANDAL C. JARRELL, managing editor
MARYANNE SNELL, director of sales & marketing

Original Queen & Country logo designed by
STEVEN BIRCH @ Servo

This collects issues 13-15 of the Oni Press comics series *Queen & Country*™.

Queen & Country is ™ & © 2002, 2003 Greg Rucka. Unless otherwise specified, all other material © 2003 Oni Press, Inc. Oni Press logo and icon are ™ & © 2003 Oni Press, Inc. All rights reserved. Oni Press logo and icon artwork created by Dave Gibbons. The events, institutions, and characters presented in this book are fictional. Any resemblance to actual persons, living or dead, is purely coincidental. No portion of this publication may be reproduced, by any means, without the express written permission of the copyright holders.

ONI PRESS, INC.
1305 SE Martin Luther King Jr. Blvd
Suite A
Portland, OR 97214

www.onipress.com

First edition: October 2003
ISBN 1-929998-68-6

3 5 7 9 10 8 6 4 2

PRINTED IN CANADA.

INTRODUCTION

by JOHN ROGERS

"What do you think?"

My wife folded over the last page of my screenplay for the film adaptation of *Queen & Country*. She nodded thoughtfully — and then chucked it at my head. It bounced cleanly off my right temple.

"YOU JERK!"

"Ow," I wittily responded.

"YOU'RE IN LOVE WITH TARA CHACE!"

Rubbing my skull, I chuckled soothingly. "Don't be ridiculous ..."

But, because we've been married for over a decade, she knew. Of course I was in love with Tara Chace.

Tara and I met in passing, while I was working out my serious crush on a certain US Marshall in Antarctica. "Lily Sharpe" zipped through the story like a breezy plot device, a smart writer's choice. "Two women in a place where women are not stereotypically found. Spiffy." But then I discovered that she had her own series, and it was a goddam *spy book*, no laser watches, no M, no arch-villians with volcano lairs. How fantastic is that? Tara Chace and her friends drive around, sweating, looking for dead-drops. She kicks blackmailers in the kneecap. She has to hustle up a toy gun, because the government won't let her have a real one. Greg knows his tradecraft. He knows the difference between a "stopper" and a "plug" in a vehicle setup. Every pore of this book oozes authenticity. The scale is big enough to be suspenseful without being ridiculous. Every mission isn't world-ending, and to me that's refreshing.

So I hopped on. I mean, it meant nothing really. Tara had a spy book, I dug spy books. Perfectly innocent. Coffee after work.

Oh, she was inscrutable at first. A hard case. But then, story after story, the cracks showed. Tara's obsessions, her failings, her hubris. One second she froze out some embassy twit with a thousand yard stare, the next she was balancing "flirty" and "menacing" with alchemical expertise in order to get what she wanted. She can vaporize a man's spine from three hundred yards, but she won't feel good about doing it. Tara Chace is a wonderfully moral character in an immoral world — the trick is, you know she's got some personal code, some line she just won't cross, you're just never sure exactly what it is. One issue, two, and you're hooked. She gives you the dead eyes. Then the smile comes. The wry joke over pints, and BOOM. You're done for. You're at her mercy.

Tara Chace can shoot, fight, drink you under the table and unravel complex terrorist plots while fighting a hangover. One could argue male readers don't fall in love with Tara because she's the *woman* we always *wanted*; we fall in love with her because she's the *man* we always *wanted to be*.

And her lads: Wallace, who would have been the heroic staff sergeant in the Great War version of the book. Wallace can't shoot worth a damn. He's a little older, a little out of shape. He is, in theory, a Very Bad Spy. But it's amazing how, regardless of which artist is covering the book, Wallace's intelligence radiates off him in waves. Wallace is the guy you want hunting the Bad Men.

Edward Kittering, in the hands of any other writer, would have been the "square-jawed recruit viewpoint character." Instead, he gets in way over his head. And fast. It's a brilliant counterpoint to Wallace, how youth and speed really don't have anything on cunning and experience in this world. Edward's relationship with Tara is ... not healthy. Not all his fault, either. Greg's not afraid to write his characters acting stupidly, selfishly, and just generally practicing the poor judgment one might expect from high-strung people working in a high-pressure job.

(This is something almost impossible to do in film. When you write that moment in a script, some pinhead in a suit will invariably say, "Why did he do that? It doesn't make sense!" To which the writer replies, " Exactly. Why DID he do that? It DOESN'T make sense!" The writer will then lean back in his chair, confident he has won the point. Silly, silly writer.)

Then, of course... Crocker. Just say the name. "Crocker." Now say it with a blend of hate and respect. "Crocker." It's the perfect mixture of syllables for the bastard whom you'd prefer didn't exist at all, but if he's going to walk the earth he might as well be on your side.

But set the cool characters, whip-smart writing and tricky little plots aside for a moment. When you peel off the top of *Queen & Country*, there are two big, BIG pieces of heavy-duty writer work being done here.

First: the tone on every story arc is consistently unheroic without being anti-heroic. This is really what sets *Queen & Country* apart for me. Tara doesn't wind up her missions on some desert island picking diamonds out of bodily orifices. She stands in the crappy rain, in a crappy alleyway in some crappy city, counting who's alive and who's dead, and that's good enough. This is important, because the world really is won by the inch. People need to read these stories. They need to understand it's the long game that counts. Every day goes by, and the world burns, and all Tara and her ilk can do is keep the flames away from the front door one more morning. Every time they do that, it's a victory. You can't win the War on Terror. You. Can. Not. You can just win today's battle.

A quick aside: this tone is directly how I wound up writing the film. The cunning Fox exec in charge of the book, Emma Watts, told me it was available. I turned it down, partly because I didn't have a solid approach off the top of my head, and partly because I was terrified of being the guy who screwed up *Queen & Country*. She kept bringing it back into my view. I'd start saying how I'd go about it, then I'd stop myself. No. Not going to take the gig.

I'd just found the DVD set for the great '70s British TV spy program *The Sandbaggers*. That show's already been discussed in the previous trades, so I'll just summarize it as I always do: "Good men in ugly suits dying badly in Prague." Not a single romantic, heroic moment in the whole dirty game, but you couldn't take your eyes off those ruthless bastards. I e-mailed Emma: "Hey, not that I'm going to write *Q&C*, but *The Sandbaggers* is totally the tone you're looking for."

Emma e-mailed back: "Greg says that's what the whole series is based on, and for you to get your ass in here and write it before I find some hack who hasn't read the book."

And so, Greg lucked out and got a hack who had read the book.

Second: in a wonderful way, Greg is using the real world of espionage as a metaphor for emotional growth. You never score the big win, you take the win you can. Don't overestimate your own importance in things. Yet never forget you can make one small difference through a single principled choice. Tara begins the series as a bit of a wreck. (Actually, I don't know if Greg intended it that way, it's what I read into the book. The screenplay runs on that supposition too, so I hope Greg gets used to the idea ...)

As Tara progresses through the Operations detailed in these trades, you can see her internalize the challenges from each Op, apply them to her own mental reconstruction of who Tara Chace is. That's a helluva stunt. Particularly because spies aren't the type to "talk their motivation," as actors say. Everything's conveyed through the telling glance, the long pause, all done in a static medium over a dozen issues. Yet go back and buy the other trades — they should be right next to this one — and you can quite clearly track emotional growth and conflict in every character, in clear arcs, over the run of the series.

Writers like Greg could bury a lot of us over here in the TV and film side. Thank God they all like living in Oregon so much. No, seriously, they all live in Oregon. It's actually kind of creepy.

I could rave on and on, but you've got the book in your hands. Don't take my word for it. In the words of *The Children's Guide to Postmodern Espionage Stories*: "See Tara. See Tara kick ass. Kick ass, Tara, Kick ass."

John Rogers
September 4, 2003

John Rogers is a screenwriter and producer living in Tinsel Town. He created and produced the popular Jackie Chan Adventures *cartoon for Kids WB and his screenplay credits included the science fiction blockbuster* The Core *and the afforementioned* Queen & Country *film currently in development with Tall Trees Productions and 20th Century Fox.*

CHAPTER 1

ROSTER

C

Ubiquitous code-name for the current head of S.I.S.. Real name is Sir Wilson Stanton Davies.

DONALD WELDON

Deputy Chief of Service, has oversight of all aspects of Intelligence gathering and operations. Immediate superior to Crocker.

PAUL CROCKER

Director of Operations encompassing all field work in all theaters of operations.

In addition to commanding individual stations, has direct command of the Special Section—sometimes referred to as Minders—used for special operations.

TOM WALLACE

Head of the Special Section, a Special Operations Officer with the designation Minder One. Responsible for the training and continued well-being of his unit, both at home and in the field. Six year veteran of the Minders.

TARA CHACE

Special Operations Officer, designated Minder Two. Entering her third year as Minder.

EDWARD KITTERING

Special Operations Officer, designated Minder Three. Has been with the Special Section for less than a year.

OPS ROOM STAFF:

ALEXIS

Mission Control Officer (also called Main Communications Officer)-responsible for maintaining communications between the Operations Room and the agents in the field.

RON

Duty Operations Officer, responsible for monitoring the status and importance of all incoming intelligence, both from foreign stations and other sources.

KATE

Personal Assistant to Paul Crocker, termed P.A. to D.Ops. Possibly the hardest and most important job in the Service.

OTHERS:

COLIN BECK

Mid-fifties self-made billionaire known for his aggressive business tactics, savvy, and willpower. Owns or has interests in technology, mass media, entertainment, and communication industries.

RACHEL BECK

Mid-twenties dilettante, currently living in Paris on a substantial allowance from her father. Aspiring fashion designer.

RENE DUPUIS

Also mid-fifties, head of IID, a company with almost three hundred years of history in France. Under Rene, IID has moved its focus from its traditional shipping and transport lines to the communications and tech industries.

PARIS.
J'ESPÈRE QUE LA CHAMBRE TE PLAÎT.
ELLE EST TRÈS BIEN.
TU VEUX BOIRE QUELQUE CHOSE? JE POURRAIS FAIRE MONTER DU CHAMPAGNE.
SI JE BOIS UN VERRE DE PLUS, JE NE TIENDRAI PLUS DEBOUT.
ÇA TOMBE BIEN...CE N'EST PAS LA POSITION QUE J'AVAIS EN TÊTE...
J'AI TELLEMENT ENVIE DE TOI, RACHEL. CA FAIT DES SEMAINES QUE J'AI ENVIE DE TOI.
A CHAQUE FOIS QUE JE TE VOIS, TU M'EXCITES, JE NE PEUX PAS M'EN EMPÊCHER.
ANDRÉ...
JE NE PENSE QU'À TE TOUCHER...
...À TE DONNER DU PLAISIR...
...À TE FAIRE L'AMOUR.

...TU AS LES MAINS TELLEMENT CHAUDES...
...OOH C'EST BON OOHHH...
VAS-Y, BOUGE COMME ÇA, REMUE TON CUL COMME ÇA
TU AIMES ÇA, HEIN? TU AIMES ÇA QUAND JE TE METS LES DOIGTS DANS LE CUL...
...DIS-MOI QUE TU AIMES AVOIR MES DOIGTS DANS LE CUL.
NHHH OOOH OUI N'ARRÊTE PAS CE QUE TU FAIS OH OUI--
--OOOH MMMM N'ARRÊTE OOOHH PAS MMMM OOHHHH MA CHÉRIE NNGGGGG MON AMOUR...
NGHH OOHHH C'EST BON OUI COMME ÇA...
...TU LA SENS, DANS TA CHATTE, QUAND JE TE BAISE COMME ÇA?
NHH OH OUI OUI COMME ÇA COMME ÇA SUR MON CLITO GNNH HHN OOH OUI TU VAS ME FAIRE JOUIR--
--JE VAIS JOUIR TELLEMENT FORT SUR TA BITE NHH
DIS-MOI, RACHEL...
JE CROYAIS QU'IL ALLAIT AU MOINS LUI DEMANDER DE LE SUCER D'ABORD.
...DIS-MOI QUE TU LA VEUX--
OOH ANDRÉ ANDRÉ HNNH JE LA VEUX, METS-LA-MOI, METS-LA-MOI--
IL LA VUI DEMANDER.
LA VIDÉO MARCHE BIEN?
--NHHH HNH HNH HNNN NHHHH OH OUI OH OUI--
IMPECCABLE...

...JE PEUX MÊME LUI COMPTER LES POILS DE LA CHATTE.
--OH OH OUI ANDRÉ GNHHHH...
...HNN AH AH AH OH CHÉRIE...
EH, OH!
ON NE FUME PAS ICI.
ELLE RISQUE DE SENTIR LA FUMÉE PAR LE TROU DU MUR.
...OH CHÉRIE OH MON AMOUR...
Y À PAS A S'INQUIÉTER, À MON AVIS.
...C'EST MON TOUR MAINTENANT...
ANTON LA TIENT PLUTÔT OCCUPÉE POUR LE MOMENT.
OOH, OH, RACHEL, CHÉRIE, TU N'ES PAS OBLIGÉE...
NE DIS RIEN... J'AI ENVIE DE LE FAIRE...

LONDON.
YOU OR ME TODAY?
ME, I THINK. YOU WENT IN FIRST LAST TWO DAYS IN A ROW.
WE COULD GO IN TOGETHER, YOU KNOW.
ARRIVING AT THE OFFICE AT THE SAME TIME, THAT DOESN'T PROVE WE'RE SLEEPING TOGETHER.
WHY TEMPT FATE?
WHY INDEED?
WE'RE ONLY SHAGGING LIKE RABBITS EVERY CHANCE WE GET.
IF YOU WANT TO GO FIRST TODAY, THAT'S FINE WITH ME, ED.
THAT'S NOT WHAT I WANT.

AN AFFAIR, BY DEFINITION, IS CONDUCTED WITH A DEGREE OF DISCRETION, IF NOT SECRECY.
IS THAT WHAT THIS IS? AN AFFAIR?
THAT WAS MY UNDERSTANDING. AM I MISTAKEN?
NO.
NO, YOU'RE NOT MISTAKEN.
THEN WHAT'S BOTHERING YOU?
NOTHING.
SEE YOU IN THE PIT.

BLOODY DAFT IS WHAT IT IS.
KEEP TALKING LIKE THAT, YOU'LL HAVE ME CONVINCED YOU REALLY DON'T WANT TO GO.
I DON'T.
CAN'T BE AS BAD AS ALL THAT, SURELY?
OBVIOUSLY YOU'VE NEVER BEEN TO WASHINGTON WITH WELDON AND THE REST OF THOSE PRATS CALLED THE JOINT INTELLIGENCE RESOURCE COMMITTEE.
A WEEK WASTED MAKING NICE WITH BLOODY POLITICOS WHO DON'T HAVE THE FIRST IDEA OF OUR OPERATIONAL NEEDS OR GOALS.
SELF -CONGRATULATORY DINNERS WHERE THE UNDER-ASSISTANT TO THE DEPUTY DIRECTOR OF INTERNAL EXCREMENT CROWS ABOUT THE COOPERATION OF THE LAST EIGHTEEN MONTHS.
JENNY DECIDED SHE'D RATHER STAY HOME, DID SHE?
YES.
DAMMIT.

KATE!
WHY THE HELL CAN'T I FIND THE LEIGHTON-DUNN BRIEF?
BECAUSE IT'S ALREADY IN YOUR BAG.
THE DEPUTY CHIEF IS WAITING FOR YOU IN THE CAR.
YES, I KNOW, THANK YOU.
IF IT'S URGENT, YOU CAN REACH ME IN D.C..
I KNOW THE DRILL.
SIMON AND C ARE BOTH IN THE BUILDING ALL WEEK, SO GO TO THEM IF YOU HAVE CONCERNS OR QUESTIONS.
BUT REMEMBER, IT'S YOUR SHOW, NOT THEIRS. YOU'RE THE ACTING DIRECTOR OF OPERATIONS IN MY ABSENCE.
YOU'RE A TRUE MOTHER-HEN, YOU KNOW THAT?
HEN-PECKED, CERTAINLY.
THE CAR--
I HEARD YOU THE FIRST TIME.
GO, PAUL. WE'LL BE FINE HERE.

LIKE PULLING TEETH TO GET HIM OUT OF HERE.
AND ONLY MARGINALLY LESS LOSS OF BLOOD.
COFFEE?
PLEASE. SIGNALS HAVE BEEN SORTED?
BUT OF COURSE...
OUR ABSENT LORD AND MASTER CAME IN AT FOUR THIS MORNING TO VET THE STACK.
CLEARED THE IMMEDIATES AND THE PRIORITIES...
...LEFT THE ROUTINES FOR YOU TO SORT.
ANYTHING OF INTEREST?
THEY'RE CALLED "ROUTINE," TOM.
IF THEY WERE INTERESTING, THEY'D BE GRADED HIGHER.

OOH, HERE'S ONE FROM PARIS.
TO: Crocker, Paul D. Director Operations
FROM: Stephenson, Mark Paris Station
COLIN BECK
CAN'T BE IMPORTANT.
NO?
NOT UNLESS THERE'S SOMEONE THEY CAN SURRENDER TO THAT I DON'T KNOW ABOUT.
YOU LOVE IT WHEN HE LEAVES, DON'T YOU?
AS I LIVE AND BREATHE.
ANYTHING ELSE?
THE INTELLIGENCE BRIEFS HAVE TO BE BACK TO D. INT THIS FORENOON, OPERATION: LANDSLIDE SHOULD WRAP UP BEFORE DARK, YOU'VE GOT TWO MINDERS IN THE PIT...
...AND WITHOUT ME THIS PLACE WOULD FALL APART.
BUT YOU KNEW THAT ALREADY.
TRUE.
THEN ALL IS RIGHT WITH THE WORLD.
LET'S HOPE IT STAYS THAT WAY.

PARIS.
THANK YOU, DENNIS.
YOU CAN KEEP IT RUNNING.
CERTAINLY, MISTER BECK.
THIS WON'T TAKE LONG. THEN WE CAN GET SOME LUNCH.
NO RUSH, DA. I'VE GOT MY TUNES.
RIGHT...

...SORRY I'M LATE. HAD A CONFERENCE CALL WITH SYDNEY THAT RAN LONG, THEN HAD TO PICK MY LITTLE GIRL UP AT HER HOTEL.
TAKING HER TO THE LOUVRE THIS AFTERNOON.
I TRUST THIS WILL BE THE LAST TIME YOU KEEP ME WAITING, MONSIEUR BECK?
I THINK SO, RENE. BUT NOT FOR ANY REASON YOU'LL LIKE.
BT CAME IN WITH ANOTHER OFFER LAST NIGHT.
UNLESS YOU CAN COUGH UP AN ADDITIONAL EIGHTY MILLION POUNDS, THERE'S NO DEAL.
THAT'S PREPOSTEROUS.
IT MAY BE, BUT IT'S ALSO WHAT THE BRITISH ARE BRINGING TO THE TABLE.
UNLESS YOU CAN BEAT IT, WE'VE GOT NOTHING MORE TO TALK ABOUT.

I WOULD LIKE TO SPEAK WITH YOU ALONE, MONSIEUR BECK.
RENE, MY DRIVER AND MY DAUGHTER ARE WAITING--
PLEASE.
AFTER ALL, YOU KEPT ME WAITING.
RIGHT, YOU LOT, GO ON.
RENE WANTS TO YELL AT ME IN PRIVATE.
IT'S MONEY, RENE; DON'T TAKE IT PERSONALLY.
YOU SHOULD LOOK AT MY COUNTER-OFFER, MONSIEUR BECK.
UNLESS IT'S ANOTHER EIGHTY-ONE MILLION, I'M NOT INTERESTED.

I THINK THIS WILL HOLD YOUR ATTENTION.
THE CD-ROM CONTAINS A COPY OF THE FULL VIDEO. THE AUDIO IS INCLUDED.
THE TRANSCRIPT IS A TRANSLATION. YOUR DAUGHTER SPEAKS SURPRISINGLY GOOD FRENCH...
...ESPECIALLY CONSIDERED WHAT WAS INSIDE OF HER AT THE TIME--
YOU PIECE OF DOGSHIT!
I'LL FUCKING SLOT YOU!

PLEASE, MONSIEUR BECK.
JUST BECAUSE YOU ARE CRUDE, YOUR LANGUAGE NEED NOT BE.
THE ONLY COPY LIES BEFORE YOU. I CONTROL THE ORIGINAL. YOU CAN HAVE IT ONCE OUR BUSINESS IS COMPLETED.
...AND SEE THAT THEY REACH YOUR COMPETITORS IN THE MEDIA.
YOU BASTARD.
IF, HOWEVER, YOU WOULD RATHER DEAL WITH BRITISH TELECOM, I WILL HAVE NO CHOICE BUT TO MAKE MORE COPIES...
NO, COLIN, I CAN ASSURE YOU THAT I KNOW THE IDENTITIES OF BOTH MY PARENTS.
I EXPECT TO SEE PRELIMINARY PAPERWORK BY THE END OF THE WEEK.
IN FUTURE, MONSIEUR BECK, PLEASE REFRAIN FROM USING MY CHRISTIAN NAME WITHOUT MY PERMISSION...

...THAT IS RESERVED FOR MY FRIENDS ALONE.
AND A MAN LIKE YOU COULD NEVER BE MY FRIEND.

TARA?
HMM?
WE SHOULD TALK. ABOUT THIS MORNING, I MEAN.
DREET DREET
NOT HERE.
YES, HERE. IT'S JUST US, TARA--
DREET DREET
NOT AT THE OFFICE, ED.
IT'S NOT LIKE YOU'LL WANT TO TALK ABOUT IT TONIGHT, EITHER, THOUGH, IS IT?
YOU LITTLE SHIT.

MINDER TWO.
...NO, TOM, I WASN'T TALKING TO YOU...
...NOTHING I CAN'T PUT *DOWN*...
...I'LL COME RIGHT UP...
...
...NO, THAT'S FINE. WON'T BE A MINUTE.
TOM SENDING YOU ON HOLIDAY?
TARA?
SOMETHING COME UP?
DAMMIT, TARA. SAY *SOMETHING*.
HE WANTS TO TALK TO ME.
OUTSIDE.

YOU WERE AT SCHOOL WITH RACHEL BECK, WEREN'T YOU?
RAY? WE SHARED A COUPLE OF CLASSES. LANGUAGES, MOSTLY. FRENCH AND GERMAN. WHY?
YOU MEET HER FATHER?
ONCE. HE TOOK A GROUP OF US DOWN TO LONDON ONE WEEKEND. DROPPED A GOOD FIFTEEN THOUSAND POUNDS ON US. FOOD, WINE, CHAUFFEURS.
EVEN HAD PERSONAL SHOPPING AT HARRODS.
I'M ASKING AGAIN, TOM. WHY?
NOTHING SINISTER. COLIN BECK WAS MENTIONED IN THE ROUTINES FROM PARIS THIS MORNING.
MARK STEPHENSON THINKS THE DGSE MAY HAVE HIM UNDER SURVEILLANCE.
THAT'S NOT WHAT I WANTED TO TALK TO YOU ABOUT.
YOU WANT TO TALK ABOUT WHAT'S GOING ON BETWEEN ME AND ED.
ARE YOU IN LOVE WITH HIM?
GOD, NO!
JESUS, TOM!
THEN END IT.
BECAUSE IF ED ISN'T ALREADY, HE WILL BE SOON.
flick

CROCKER KNOWS SOMETHING'S GOING ON, TARA. IF HE THINKS IT'S AN OPERATIONAL LIABILITY, HE'LL HAVE YOU BOTH OUT ON YOUR EARS.
IT'S NOT AN OPERATIONAL--
MAYBE NOT FOR YOU, BUT CAN YOU SAY THE SAME FOR HIM?
ED'S A BLOODY ROMANTIC, TARA...
...YOU KEEP BUMPING YOUR UGLY BITS, HE'LL TRY TO MAKE AN HONEST WOMAN OUT OF YOU
NOT SURE THAT'S EVEN POSSIBLE, TOM.
I JUST WAS SO TIRED OF BEING ALONE, YOU KNOW?
MORE THAN YOU CAN IMAGINE.

PUB

YOU WANTED TO SEE ME, SIR?
TOM, YES, THANKS FOR COMING SO PROMPTLY.
NOT ENTIRELY CERTAIN HOW TO HANDLE THIS, AND WITH PAUL AWAY, I'M AFRAID IT FALLS TO YOU.
THIS IS COLIN BECK.
COLIN, THIS IS THE ACTING DIRECTOR OF OPERATIONS, TOM WALLACE.
AND HE CAN HELP WITH MY PROBLEM?
WHAT PROBLEM IS THAT, EXACTLY, MISTER BECK?
LONG VERSION IS IN THIS ENVELOPE...
...THE SHORT VERSION IS THAT I'M BEING BLACKMAILED BY THE FRENCH GOVERNMENT.

CHAPTER 2

PARIS.
HOTEL
<GOOD MORNING, ANTON.>
thap
<I TRUST YOU SLEPT WELL.>
<I ALWAYS SLEEP WELL.>
<THOUGH NOT ALWAYS ALONE.>
<IT'S WHAT YOU PAY ME FOR, ISN'T IT?>
<SPEAKING OF WHICH...>
<...YOU'LL FIND SOME EXTRA INSIDE. A BONUS FOR A JOB WELL DONE.>
<I'M DELIGHTED YOU'RE PLEASED.>

<I MUST ADMIT, I ENJOYED RACHEL'S COMPANY.>
<IT WAS EASY TO MAKE LOVE TO HER.>
<SHE'S... UNIQUE, IF YOU KNOW WHAT I MEAN.>
<BEAUTIFUL, INTELLIGENT, FUNNY.>
<IT DOESN'T HURT THAT SHE'S RICH, EITHER.>
<YOU'RE THINKING WITH YOUR COCK, ANTON.>
<YOU KNOW TH SITUATIO YOU CANN SEE HER E AGAIN.>
<OF COURSE I KNOW THAT!>
<YOU KNOW WHAT YOU SHOULD DO, MY FRIEND? GET OUT OF TOWN FOR A WHILE. GO TO MONACO, OR GREECE.>
<SOMEPLACE WHERE YOU CAN FIND SOME BEAUTIFUL YOUNG THING TO SPEND YOUR MONEY ON.>

<I'M GLAD TO HEAR YOU SAY SO.>
<THINGS ARE **DELICATE** RIGHT NOW. YOUR PRESENCE COULD **COMPROMISE** OUR **OPERATION.**>
<IT'S JUST A **PITY,** THAT'S ALL I MEAN TO SAY.>
<SOMEONE WHO WILL WRAP HER EGS AROUND YOU AND HELP YOU FORGET RACHEL BECK.>
<PERHAPS YOU'RE RIGHT.>
<OF COURSE I'M RIGHT.>
<YES, WELL...IT WAS GOOD TO SEE YOU, PHILIPPE.>
<LET ME KNOW IF YOU HAVE ANY OTHER **JOBS** FOR ME.>
<WE WILL, ANTON, DON'T WORRY.>
<HE THINKS HE'S IN **LOVE.**>
<SO IT WOULD SEEM.>
<CALL THE **OFFICE,** CLAUDE...>
<...MAKE CERTAIN WE HAVE SOMEONE **WATCHING** OUR FRIEND ANTON.>
<WE DON'T WANT HIM SUFFERING FROM A SUDDEN ATTACK OF **CONSCIENCE.**>

LONDON.
Operations
Head of Section
Chace, T.
Kittering, E.

MORNING.
MORNING.
RAYBURN CAME BY WITH YOUR KASHMIR BRIEF.
HE SAYS HE AGREES WITH YOUR CONCLUSIONS, AND THAT HE'LL SIGN-OFF ON THE RECOMMENDATION WITH A REVISION.
RIGHT. THANKS.
DON'T MENTION IT.

RIGHT, LISA...
AUDIO & VISUAL ANALYSIS D-17 B
Greek, L.
Hines, I.
...WHAT CAN YOU TELL ME?
IT'S AUTHENTIC.
YOU'RE CERTAIN?
ISOBEL?
AS CERTAIN AS WE CAN BE. THERE'S NO VARIATION IN ESTABLISHED SHADOWS OR OTHER AMBIENT LIGHTING...
...NO ARTIFACTING OR OTHER IMAGE DEGRADATION THAT ONE FINDS IN DOCTORED VIDEO.
THEN THERE'S THE AUDIO.
PUT THESE ON.
IT'S IN FRENCH, ISN'T IT? I WON'T UNDERSTAND A BLOODY WORD.
YOU'RE NOT LISTENING FOR CONTENT, TOM...
...YOU'RE LISTENING FOR TIMING.
THERE'S NO OVERDUB, NO LAG.
IT'S LEGITIMATE. THIS IS A RECORDING OF ACTUAL EVENTS.
DAMN.
ALL IS NOT LOST, MISTER WALLACE...

...WE RAN "ANDRE" HERE THROUGH THE VISUAL DATABASE, LOOKING TO MATCH HIS FACE WITH ANY ON FILE.
DON'T TELL ME IT ACTUALLY WORKED?
HEAVENS, NO. IT NEVER DOES.
THE COMPUTER ALWAYS WANTS TO MATCH THE SUBJECT WITH THE LATE QUEEN MOTHER, MAY SHE REST IN PEACE.
SO WHY SHOW ME "ANDRE," HERE?
WHILE WE WERE SELECTING THE CAPTURES FOR THE SEARCH, WE NOTICED SOMETHING.
TAKE A LOOK.
THAT BASTARD.
HE KNOWS HE'S ON CAMERA.

CHRIST, IT'S LIKE A MORGUE IN HERE.
LEAST AS COLD AS ONE.
AND WHAT BRINGS YOU DOWNSTAIRS, TOM? YOU GET LONELY PLAYING D. OPS ALL BY YOURSELF?
I THOUGHT A VISIT WITH YOU PEASANTS WAS IN ORDER.
WHAT'S THIS?
DIRTY PICTURES OF AN OLD FRIEND.
OOH, CAN I SEE?
TWO QUESTIONS. FIRST, WHO TOOK IT?
SECOND, WHO'S THE MAN?

AND FOR THOSE OF US JOINING LATE, A THIRD. WHO'S THE BIRD?
HER NAME IS RACHEL BECK. AND YES, SHE'S THAT RACHEL BECK.
TOM?
ACCORDING TO COLIN BECK--WHO IS UPSTAIRS IN C'S OFFICE AT THIS MOMENT--THE ANSWER TO QUESTION THE FIRST IS THE FRENCH GOVERNMENT.
THE DGSE, SPECIFICALLY.
QUESTION TWO, NO IDEA. BUT WHOEVER HE IS, HE KNEW HE WAS ON CAMERA AT THE TIME.
AND SHE DIDN'T?
NO, IT LOOKS LIKE A HONEY-TRAP.
BECK CLAIMS THE FRENCH ARE TRYING TO BLACKMAIL HIM.
POOR RACHEL.
THOUGHT YOU MIGHT SAY THAT.
RIGHT, C'MON.
LET'S GIVE HER OLD MAN THE BAD NEWS.

MY APOLOGIES FOR THE *DELAY*, SIR...
...BUT I WANTED THE *LAB* TO *AUTHENTICATE* THE MATERIAL BEFORE WE DETERMINED HOW TO PROCEED.
PRESUMABLY THEY *HAVE* DONE?
YES, SIR. CREEK IS *CERTAIN* IT'S REAL.
SO I'M *STUCK*. THESE FRENCH *BASTARDS* ARE HOLDING MY DAUGHTER'S *PRIVACY* HOSTAGE.
BAD *ENOUGH* YOUR *LOT* ARE *LEERING* AT RACHEL. IF I DON'T GIVE THAT ARROGANT SHIT DUPUIS HIS *DEAL*, I'LL HAVE THE WESTERN *WORLD* DOING IT, AS WELL.

MISTER BECK, THIS IS SPECIAL OPERATIONS OFFICER TARA--
--CHACE? *NOT* RAY'S *MATE* FROM CAMBRIDGE?
CHRIST ON A SPIT, MY *DAUGHTER'S* SPENT THE LAST FIVE YEARS PLAYING *NOUVEAU-RICHE* IN PARIS, MEANWHILE *YOU'VE* BECOME A BLOODY *SPY*?
IT'S NICE TO SEE YOU AGAIN, SIR.
SIR? YOU USED TO CALL ME *COLIN*, TARA.
STILL HAVE THOSE TARTED-UP KNICKERS FROM RIGBY AND PELLER?
I'M WEARING THEM AS WE SPEAK.
WHAT THEY *COST*, YOU SHOULD BE.

DELIGHTFUL THOUGH IT IS TO SEE TARA AGAIN, WE'RE STILL LEFT WITH MY--AND HER MAJESTY'S GOVERNMENT'S --PROBLEM.

THE FRENCH GET THIS DEAL, HMG WILL LOSE SOMEWHERE IN THE NEIGHBORHOOD OF FIVE HUNDRED MILLION POUNDS OVER THE NEXT FIVE YEARS.
AND WITH YOUR DAUGHTER'S DIGNITY AT STAKE--
I WON'T FIGHT IT. I WON'T LET THE FRENCH HUMILIATE HER.
PLEASE UNDERSTAND ME, SIR WILSON. RACHEL'S A SPOILED MINX, BUT SHE'S MY DAUGHTER, AND I ADORE HER.
I'M NO FOOL. I'M WELL-AWARE WHAT'S SAID ABOUT ME BEHIND MY BACK.
IT DOESN'T MATTER HOW MUCH MONEY I HAVE, I'LL NEVER CRACK THE UPPER-CRUST.
BUT RAY LIVES AND DIES WITH THE REST OF THE SLOANE RANGERS, AND I WON'T SEE THEM LAUGHING AT HER.
NO MORE THAN THEY DO ALREADY, AT LEAST.

IT MIGHT HELP IF WE KNEW THE EXACT NATURE OF THIS DEAL YOU'VE BEEN REFERRING TO.
IT'S A MEDIA ARRANGEMENT, PACKAGE DEALING, ONLINE SERVICES, DIGITAL CABLE, MOBILE, ALL OF IT.
WE'RE NEGOTIATING FOR THE BEST LOCATION, AND THAT'S THE PLUM...
...BECAUSE WHEREVER WE LAND, WE'LL BE BOOSTING THE ECONOMY, AND BRING NEW REVENUE TO THE GOVERNMENT IN THE FORM OF TAXES, EMPLOYMENT, THE LIKE.
WE WERE ABOUT TO CLOSE THE DEAL, BUILD IN THE MIDLANDS. THEN THE FRENCH PULLED THIS.

YOU'RE CERTAIN IT IS THE FRENCH GOVERNMENT AND NOT SOMETHING DUPUIS COOKED UP ON HIS OWN?
NO, IT'S THE GOVERNMENT, MISTER WALLACE...
...RENE DUPUIS HAS CONNECTIONS AS MUCH AS I DO.
THE DIFFERENCE IS THAT HIS ARE FAMILY AND STRETCH BACK SIX HUNDRED YEARS, AND I'M A NEW-MONEY BASTARD WHO'S ACTUALLY EARNED HIS CLINK.
FORGET ABOUT RACHEL. THIS APPEALS TO THE NATIONAL INTEREST.
INDEED. I RECEIVED A DIRECTIVE FROM DOWNING STREET THIS MORNING TO JUST THAT EFFECT.

I THINK WE HAVE ENOUGH TO GET STARTED, COLIN.
I'LL HAVE SOMEONE SEE YOU OUT.
I APPRECIATE IT, SIR WILSON.
I'M IN LONDON FOR THE REST OF THE WEEK, MY PLACE IN MAYFAIR.

YOU CAN REACH ME THERE.

ALL RIGHT, TOM. WHAT DO WE DO NOW?
IT'S NOT TECHNICALLY A SPECIAL OP, SIR. BUT WITH YOUR PERMISSION, I'D LIKE TO SEND MINDER TWO TO PARIS.
TARA HAS A RELATIONSHIP WITH RACHEL BECK, AND I THINK THAT WILL HELP US SORT FACT FROM SPECULATION.
WE WERE AT CAMBRIDGE TOGETHER, SIR.
I SEE. SO YOU'LL SPEAK TO MISS BECK. TO WHAT END?
MINDER TWO WILL ATTEMPT TO IDENTIFY AND LOCATE THE MAN IN THE VIDEO. CREEK'S ANALYSIS IS THAT WHOEVER HE IS, HE KNEW THEY WERE ON CAMERA.

PRESUMABLY EMPLOYED BY THE DGSE TO SEDUCE MISS BECK?
IF WE CAN GET CONFIRMATION, WE CAN DECIDE ON FURTHER ACTION.
CAN YOU COUNT ON HER HELP? FOR THAT MATTER, DOES SHE EVEN KNOW ABOUT THE VIDEO?
I THINK I CAN APPEAL TO HER AS A FRIEND, SIR.
IF I HAVE TO, I'LL TELL HER ABOUT THE FILM.

COLIN WON'T LIKE THAT.
VERY WELL. KEEP ME POSTED.

SHOULD I HEAD TO THE OPS ROOM FOR AN OFFICIAL BRIEFING?
NAH, I'LL HANDLE THAT END. YOU JUST GET YOURSELF TO PARIS.
YOU KNOW, CROCKER WAS HERE, HE'D NEVER AUTHORIZE THE OP.
HE'D SCREAM ABOUT THE GOVERNMENT USING THE MINDERS FOR THEIR OWN PRIVATE AFFAIRS.
YOU HEARD C. DOWNING STREET WANTS IT DONE.
OF COURSE THEY DO. COLIN BECK IS A MAJOR MONEY PLAYER.
ISSUES OF HIS IMPACT ON THE ECONOMY NOTWITHSTANDING.
CAN YOU IMAGINE BEING THAT RICH?
NO. I GET AS FAR AS THE PRIVATE JET AND GO SLACK-JAWED.
NO KIDDING.
"TARTED-UP KNICKERS"?
SHUT UP, TOM.

PARIS.
I HAVE A DELIVERY FOR MISS BECK.
WHO IS IT?
LEAVE IT WITH THE CONCIERGE.
I'M SORRY, BUT I NEED YOUR SIGNATURE.
JUST A SECOND--
--TEE?
OH MY GOD, TEE!
HELLO, RAY.
BLOODY HELL IT'S GOOD TO SEE YOU! HOW LONG HAS IT BEEN, IT'S BEEN AGES! WHAT'RE YOU DOING IN PARIS?
COME IN, COME IN!
THIS IS SUCH THE TOTAL SURPRISE, FUCKING BRILLIANT. COME ON IN!
THANKS.

GOD, IT'S BEEN, WHAT, THREE YEARS?
ABOUT THAT, YES.
HOW'D YOU FIND ME? LAST WE TALKED YOU WERE JUST GOING INTO THE FOREIGN OFFICE.
STILL PUSHING PAPER FOR SOME UNDER-SECRETARY?
PRETTY MUCH.
I RAN INTO YOUR FATHER LAST WEEK, HE SAID YOU WERE LIVING IN PARIS NOW. I WAS DUE SOME TIME, THOUGHT I'D NIP OVER AND SEE YOU.
YOU SAW DA? ISN'T HE A HOOT?
HE WAS ALWAYS KEEN ON YOU, YOU KNOW? DIDN'T LIKE MOST OF MY OTHER FRIENDS, BUT HE LIKED YOU.
DIDN'T HE OFFER YOU A JOB AFTER CAMBRIDGE?
THE ROAD NOT TAKEN.
I'M SURPRISED I FOUND YOU AT HOME.
I THOUGHT FOR CERTAIN YOU'D BE OUT ON THE TOWN, RUNNING WITH THE IN-CROWD AND ALL.
IT'S THE OFF-SEASON, TEE. THEY'VE DECAMPED FOR SWITZERLAND OR THE CARIBBEAN.
BUT YOU'RE HERE? MUST BE A LAD, THEN. MUST BE A HELL OF A LAD.

TEE, STOP.
OH MY GOD, I'M RIGHT. I'M RIGHT, YOU'VE GOT YOURSELF A BOY!
C'MON, TELL ME ABOUT HIM. WHAT'S HIS NAME?
ANDRE, AND THAT'S ALL I'M SAYING RIGHT NOW.
LET'S GO OUT, LET'S GET A MEAL AND THEN GET PISSED...
...AND WHEN WE'RE GOOD AND DRUNK I'LL TELL YOU ALL ABOUT ANDRE...
...AND YOU CAN TELL ME ABOUT WHOEVER IT IS YOU'VE GOT RATTLING YOUR FILLINGS AT NIGHT.

SOUNDS LIKE A PERFECT PLAN, RAY.

WHAT'RE YOU STILL DOING HERE?
MY JOB, LAST I CHECKED.
IT'S TOO LATE IN THE DAY TO BE A COMEDIAN, ED.

C'MON, I'LL BUY YOU A PINT.
I THINK YOU'VE DONE MORE THAN ENOUGH, TOM.
DAS PIT

I'LL BE OVER AT THE PUB...
...YOU HAVE SOMETHING YOU NEED TO SAY TO ME, YOU CAN SAY IT TO ME THERE.

...TELL ME HE DIDN'T!
TRUTH! HE HAD A ROOM AT THE RITZ, HE'D PAID FOR IT HIMSELF...
...GOD, TEE, YOU HAVE NO IDEA HOW REFRESHING THAT WAS!
FINALLY, A MAN WHO DOESN'T EXPECT MY FATHER TO PAY FOR EVERYTHING!
POOR LITTLE RAY, IT'S SO HARD TO BE RICH, ISN'T IT?
IT IS!
WELL, ALL RIGHT, IT ISN'T.
BUT IT'S NICE WHEN THAT ISN'T THE ONLY REASON A MAN'S TALKING TO YOU.
SURE.
YOU KNOW WHY I'M HERE, TARA? WHY I'M NOT IN BERNE OR CAYMAN?
YOU HATE TO SKI AND YOU BURN EASILY?
BITCH!
CAREFUL! I BRUISE VERY EASILY!
I'M IN LOVE, THAT'S WHY I'M HERE.
I LOVE HIM, AND WHAT'S BETTER IS THAT HE LOVES ME....

THE GORDON PUB
THE GORDON PUB
YOU GOING TO *THROW* IT AT ME LIKE A *BOY*, OR TAKE A *SEAT* LIKE A *MAN*?
WHY'D YOU MAKE HER DO IT, TOM? WHY COULDN'T YOU LEAVE IT *ALONE*?

I DIDN'T MAKE TARA DO ANYTHING, ED.
SHE DUMPED YOU FOR HER REASONS ALONE.
I TRIED TO WARN YOU CLEAR, YOU WEREN'T HAVING ANY.
IT'D BE DIFFERENT IF YOU WERE WORKING FOR RAYBURN, OR EVEN ON A STATION.
YOU'RE JUST LUCKY IT'S OVER BEFORE CROCKER FELT THE NEED TO SAY SOMETHING.
I DON'T CARE ABOUT THAT.
TARA DOES.

I HATE THIS JOB.

YOU SEEING ANYONE?
I WAS.
JUST ENDED IT, IN FACT.
NOT WELL, I'M AFRAID.
WHY'D YOU END IT?
I WAS USING HIM.
EVERYONE USES EVERYONE, TEE.
WAY OF THE WORLD, ISN'T IT?
LET'S JUST SAY MY HEART WASN'T IN IT.
SO THIS ANDRE MARION OF YOURS, WHEN DO I GET TO MEET HIM?
YOU ALMOST MET HIM TONIGHT. HE WAS SUPPOSED TO COME OVER.
HE CALLED THIS AFTERNOON, SAID HE HAD TO GO OUT OF TOWN, SOME BUSINESS IN CANNES.
HE'S AN ACTOR, DID I TELL YOU?
NO, YOU HADN'T MENTIONED IT.

HE SAY WHEN HE'D BE BACK?
NO. HE WAS SUPPOSED TO CALL TONIGHT, THOUGH.
BONSOIR, MADAME SERNETT.
BONSOIR, MADEMOISELLE.
YOU WANT TO COME UP?
HMM?
NO, I DON'T THINK SO. TOO MUCH WINE, IF I DON'T GET BACK TO MY HOTEL I'LL FALL ASLEEP ON THE STAIRS, I'M AFRAID.
CALL TOMORROW, THEN? I KNOW A PLACE WE CAN HAVE LUNCH.
ABSOLUTELY.
GREAT TO SEE YOU, TEE.
HAVE A GOOD NIGHT.
PEK
YOU AS WELL.

TU SAIS QU'ELLE TE CROIT À CANNES?
ELLE CROIT MÊME QU'ELLE VA TE REVOIR.
MAIS ON SAIT BIEN QUE NON, HEIN?
NOUS SAVONS TOUS LES DEUX CE QUE TU LUI AS FAIT.
NOUS SAVONS TOUS LES DEUX CE QUI VA SE PASSER MAINTENANT.
DON'T WE, "ANDRE"?

CHAPTER 3

YOU DON'T MIND IF WE DO THIS IN ENGLISH, DO YOU?
MY FRENCH IS A TAD CREAKY.
YOU SMOKE?
DO I--? NO, I DO NOT SMOKE--
YOU DO NOW. ASK ME FOR A CIGARETTE.
RACHEL'S BEEN WAITING FOR YOU, ANDRE.
NOT TERRIBLY GENTLEMANLY TO KEEP HER WAITING LIKE THAT.
I KNOW.
YOU'RE BEING FOLLOWED, YOU KNOW THAT, ANDRE?
WHAT?
TWO OF THEM...
...ACROSS THE STREET.

DO YOU SUPPOSE THEY SMOKE?
DO THEY-- I DON'T UNDERSTAND--
NEVER MIND.
I THINK WE SHOULD TALK, ANDRE.
NO. NO, I REALLY CAN'T.
I THINK YOU CAN.
I THINK YOU WANT TO.
WHY ELSE ARE YOU HANGING AROUND RACHEL'S APARTMENT?
I HAVE TO GO.
NOT YET.
PLEASE, MADAME, GET OUT OF MY WAY.
WHAT ARE YOU AFRAID OF, ANDRE?
I CANNOT SPEAK WITH YOU.
LITTLE LATE FOR THAT FEAR, DON'T YOU THINK?

EXCUSE ME--
YOU'RE NOT HEARING ME, ANDRE...
...YOU CAN'T LEAVE.
HEY!
WHAT'S GOING ON?
IT'S NO CONCERN OF YOURS.
I THINK IT IS. I THINK YOU SHOULD LEAVE OUR FRIEND ALONE.
COME ALONG, ANTON.
IT'S NOT HOW IT LOOKS--
--SHE JUST STARTED TALKING TO ME, I WASN'T--

--NO!
GHNNN
HKKK
BITCH!
HNNNU
AHH!

AHHHH!
GHUHHNN
NHUHUHHuu
S'IL VOUS PLAIT--
NO.

WE'RE GOING TO HAVE A CHAT.
JESUS CHRIST, DO YOU HAVE ANY IDEA WHAT YOU'VE DONE TO ME?
DO YOU KNOW WHAT HAPPENS WHEN THEY FIND OUT?
THEY'RE GOING TO BLAME ME FOR THIS!
GOD, I WASN'T EVEN SUPPOSED TO BE HERE...
YET HERE YOU ARE.
LOOKS LIKE YOU'RE IN A SPOT OF TROUBLE, ANDRE.
ALMOST AS BAD AS THE SPOT RACHEL'S IN, HMM?
FORTUNATE FOR YOU THAT I'M HERE.
FORTUNATE THAT YOU WANT A CHANCE TO MAKE THINGS RIGHT.
COME ALONG.
WATCH YOUR STEP.
UHNNN

HERE, THIS'LL HELP.
DRINK UP.
MERCI.
SO WHICH IS IT? ANTON OR ANDRE?
HILTON

ANTON. ANTON ROUX.

ANDRE MARION IS THE, HOW DO YOU SAY, WORK NAME?
WORK NAME, YES.
THE D.G.S.E. GAVE YOU THE WHOLE IDENTITY?
ALL RIGHT, LET'S TRY THIS ANOTHER WAY.

THESE ARE THE THINGS THAT I KNOW.
THREE DAYS AGO, YOU TOOK RACHEL BECK TO A ROOM AT THE RITZ. A ROOM YOU HAD RESERVED IN ADVANCE.
A ROOM IN WHICH YOU KNEW THERE WAS AT LEAST ONE CAMERA.
AND WHILE THAT CAMERA WAS RUNNING, YOU TOOK RACHEL BECK TO BED...
...AND YOU DID EVERYTHING IN YOUR POWER TO MAKE HER LOOK LIKE A WHORE.
NON, NO, IT WAS NOT LIKE THAT--

SURE HOW IT LOOKS, ANTON. I'VE SEEN THE VIDEO, AND YOU WERE QUITE THE COMMANDING LOVER.
SHE WAS SHAMELESS, SHE WAS SO EAGER TO MAKE LOVE TO YOU.
I DON'T THINK THERE'S ANYTHING SHE WOULDN'T HAVE DONE, HAD YOU ASKED HER.
AND YOU DID, DIDN'T YOU?
THING ABOUT VIDEO, IT CAN'T TELL THE DIFFERENCE BETWEEN LOVE AND SEX.
WHEN THAT FILM GETS SHOWN, THE AUDIENCE WON'T BE ABLE TO TELL, EITHER.
YOU KNEW HOW SHE FELT, AND YOU ABUSED IT. YOU USED HER FOR SHOW, AND YOU GOT OFF ON IT.
YOU TOLD HER YOU LOVED HER, YOU TOLD HER SHE MEANT EVERYTHING, AND THEN YOU LET YOUR FRIENDS IN THE D.G.S.E. RECORD IT ALL WHILE YOU FUCKED HER LIKE SO MUCH MEAT.
SO, YES, ANTON...
...YOU MADE HER INTO A WHORE, AND YOU DID IT FOR THE WORLD TO SEE.
MUST'VE MADE YOU FEEL LIKE QUITE THE MAN.

THAT'S NOT...
...THAT'S NOT WHAT IT WAS.
THAT'S NOT WHAT IT WAS.
YOU'RE GOING TO TRY AND CONVINCE ME YOU ACTUALLY CARE ABOUT HER?
DON'T WASTE MY TIME, ANTON.
IT'S NOT WHAT YOU THINK!
AND I DON'T HAVE TO STAY HERE AND LISTEN TO YOU--

SHUT UP.

SHE'S MY FRIEND, YOU SACK OF SHIT.
RACHEL BECK IS MY FRIEND AND SHE FELL IN LOVE WITH YOU.
AND YOU USED HER.

MY FRIEND FELL IN LOVE WITH YOU, ANTON...
...AND THAT'S THE ONLY REASON I HAVEN'T STARTED PUTTING MY FAGS OUT ON YOUR FACE.
WHAT ARE YOU GOING TO DO WITH ME?
I HAVEN'T DECIDED YET.
TO TELL YOU THE HONEST TRUTH, ANTON, I WOULDN'T MIND BEATING YOU UNTIL YOU PISSED BLOOD.
YOU DON'T DOUBT THAT I CAN DO THAT, DO YOU?
NON, NO, NOT AT ALL.
GOOD.

EH, OH!
RELAX. MUCH AS I'D ENJOY HURTING YOU...
...IT WON'T SOLVE THE PROBLEM.
GET UP. TAKE THE NEWSPAPER.
SIT. HOLD THE PAPER SO I CAN SEE THE DATE.
YOU'RE GOING TO MAKE A CONFESSION. WHO HIRED YOU, WHAT THEY TOLD YOU TO DO, AND WHO YOU DID IT TO...
WHAT YOU WERE PAID. YOU'RE GOING TO GIVE THE TIMES AND THE PLACES.
ALL OF IT.
THIS CONFESSION ...IT IS NOT LEGAL.
Le Monde
IT WILL BE WORTHLESS IN COURT.
18 MARS 2003
Le
DO I LOOK LIKE THE POLICE, ANTON?
START BY GIVING YOUR REAL NAME AND YOUR DATE OF BIRTH...

...CONTACTED BY PHILIPPE GOURGEON AND CLAUDE BRETON IN FEBRUARY OF THIS YEAR...
HILTON
...PAID ME TO STRIKE UP AN INTIMATE RELATIONSHIP WITH RACHEL BECK, COLIN BECK'S DAUGHTER.
THEY TOLD ME THAT I WAS TO BRING HER TO THE RITZ ON THE NIGHT OF MARCH 15TH, TO ROOM 1822, AND THEN MAKE LOVE TO HER.
MONSIEUR GOURGEON EXPLAINED THAT THERE WOULD BE A CAMERA PLACED ABOVE THE HEADBOARD TO RECORD OUR... ACTIVITY...
HE SAID IT WAS IMPORTANT THAT I MAKE CERTAIN MADEMOISELLE BECK FACED THE CAMERA AS MUCH AS POSSIBLE...
MONSIEUR BRETON SUGGESTED...THERE WERE SPECIFIC ACTS HE WANTED MADEMOISELLE BECK TO PERFORM FOR THE CAMERA, AND I WAS INSTRUCTED TO ENCOURAGE HER--
DEET
I FELL IN LOVE WITH HER.

DO YOU HEAR ME? I SAID--
I HEARD YOU, ANTON.
IS THAT...
...ARE WE FINISHED?
WE'RE FINISHED.
WAIT!
WHAT...
...WHAT DO I DO NOW?
SHOOT YOURSELF.

LONDON.
...ANOTHER SET OF COPIES BEING MADE IN THE LAB AS WE SPEAK.
I SUSPECT THAT, SHOULD YOU PRESENT ONE TO MONSIEUR DUPUIS, HE'LL RECANT HIS THREAT TO BLACKMAIL YOUR DAUGHTER, MISTER BECK.
ACCORDING TO OUR DIRECTOR INTELLIGENCE, THE DGSE AGENTS ROUX NAMED ON THE TAPE WORK FOR JACQUES KRIEF'S DIRECTORATE.
DUPUIS AND KRIEF ARE KNOWN TO BE FRIENDS.
BRILLIANT! JUST BRILLIANT, SIR WILSON.
I'M NOT SURE I CAN THANK YOU ENOUGH, BUT I'LL DAMN WELL TRY!
THE FOREIGN SECRETARY AND I SHARE THE SAME CLUB. I'LL BE MAKING A POINT TO TELL HIM WHAT A TURN YOU'VE DONE ME NEXT CHANCE I GET.
IT WAS IN THE NATION'S INTEREST, COLIN.
IF ANYONE DESERVES THE PRAISE, IT'S MISTER WALLACE AND MISS CHACE.
TARA, MOSTLY, TO BE HONEST.

RACHEL HAS NO IDEA HOW GOOD A FRIEND YOU ARE, DOES SHE?
I WAS JUST DOING MY JOB, MISTER BECK.
COLIN.
YOU USED TO CALL ME COLIN.
YOU MIGHT WANT TO GET YOUR DAUGHTER OUT OF FRANCE, MISTER BECK. AT LEAST UNTIL YOU'VE COMPLETED YOUR BUSINESS.
JUST TO BE ON THE SAFE SIDE.
RIGHT, YES, GOOD IDEA.
HEADED TO PARIS ANYWAY, NEED TO DROP THE BOMB ON DUPUIS.
I'LL SCOOP HER UP ON THE WAY BACK.
JUST BRILLIANT.
BLOODY BRILLIANT.
WHAT A TIRESOME MAN.

HELLO, ED.
WHAT DO YOU WANT, TARA?
CAN I COME IN?
IF YOU'RE LONELY, I'M SURE YOU CAN FIND SOMEONE DOWN THE PUB.
WHY DON'T YOU SHOVE OFF AND LEAVE ME BE?
I THINK THAT WAS A LITTLE MUCH.
I THINK THAT WAS A LOT MUCH, ACTUALLY.
YEAH.

COME OUT OF THE RAIN, AT LEAST.
THANK YOU.
YOU'RE ALONE?
THAT'S A DAMN STUPID QUESTION.
THIS WAS A BAD IDEA, I'LL LEAVE YOU ALONE.
NO, SORRY, THAT WAS...
...LOOK, I'M SORRY.
WHY ARE YOU HERE?
I OWE YOU AN APOLOGY.
FOR DITCHING ME THE WAY YOU DID?
FOR WAITING SO LONG BEFORE I DID IT.

I'M IN LOVE WITH YOU.
BUT YOU KNOW THAT, DON'T YOU?
YES.

WELL, GOOD WE GOT THAT SORTED, THEN, DON'T YOU THINK?
WAS THERE SOMETHING ELSE, OR...?
ED, WE'VE STILL GOT TO WORK TOGETHER.
WE NEED TO TALK ABOUT THIS.
NO, WE REALLY DON'T, TARA.
I LOVE YOU, YOU DON'T LOVE ME, THAT'S THE MATCH.
UNLESS YOU'VE COME HERE TO TELL ME I'M WRONG.
HAVE YOU COME HERE TO TELL ME I'M WRONG?

NO.

THEN WE'RE DONE. BUT THANKS FOR POPPING BY.
ED.
YOU'RE WORRIED ABOUT THE JOB. DON'T BE.
YOU'RE A PROFESSIONAL, I'M ONE TOO.
IF NOTHING ELSE, TARA, YOU TAUGHT ME HOW TO LEAVE THE PERSONAL AT HOME.
NOW, IF YOU DON'T MIND, GRAHAM NORTON'S ABOUT TO START.

SEE YOU TOMORROW.
YOU, AS WELL.
ED--

NOKNOKNOKNOKNOK
NOKNOKNOKNOKNOK
RAY? THIS IS A SURPRISE.
COME IN.
HOW'D YOU FIND WHERE I LIVE?
OH, YOU KNOW DA AND HIS CONNECTIONS.
GOT INTO TOWN THIS EVENING, TRIED TO LOOK YOU UP.
YOU'RE NOT LISTED, YOU KNOW THAT? DA HAD TO CALL SOMEONE AT THE HOME OFFICE.
I'M SORRY TO COME BY SO LATE.

I JUST... I NEEDED TO SEE A FRIEND...
OF COURSE.
RAY? WHAT'S WRONG?
OH GOD, TEE.
IT'S JUST... IT'S SUCH A MESS, EVERYTHING'S A MESS, MY WHOLE LIFE...
...THERE'S THIS TAPE, MY FATHER HAS THIS TAPE AND ANDRE'S ON IT. HE'S IN THIS HOTEL ROOM AND THE THINGS HE'S SAYING...
GOD, TEE, THE THINGS HE'S SAYING...
IT'S ALL RIGHT, RAY, COME ON, SIT DOWN.
BUT IT'S NOT, IT'S NOT!
HE TOLD ME HE LOVED ME AND HE'S ON THIS TAPE, SAYING IT WAS FOR MONEY, THAT HE WAS PAID TO DO IT...
...THEY PAID HIM TO DO IT, SO THEY COULD TAKE PICTURES OF US...
...THEY TOOK PICTURES OF US, OF WHAT WE DID THAT NIGHT...
...IT'S ALL A MESS, IT'S ALL A LIE...

...HE NEVER LOVED ME...
...NO ONE WILL EVER LOVE ME...
...NO ONE....

PRODUCTION GALLERY

J. Alexander cover for this volume from pencil sketch to painting-in-progress.

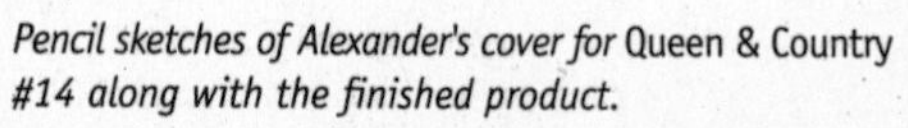

Pencil sketches of Alexander's cover for Queen & Country *#14 along with the finished product.*

Pencil drawing mocked-up in Photoshop during the design stages of the production of the Queen & Country *#15 cover.*

GREG RUCKA

Born in San Francisco, Greg Rucka was raised on the Monterey Peninsula. He is the author of several novels, including four about bodyguard Atticus Kodiak, and several comic books, for which he has won two Eisner Awards. He resides in Portland, Oregon, with his wife, Jennifer, and their children, Elliot and Dashiell.

J. ALEXANDER

J. Alexander currently resides alone in North Carolina.

He's spent the last six years working in the comics industry on series for Dark Horse Comics, Oni Press, Image Comics, Harris Comics, and Sirius Entertainment. His illustrations have been seen in adaptations of *Alice and Wonderland*, *Alice Through the Looking Glass*, and *The Time Machine* for Dalmatian Press. He's also completed many illustrations for White Wolf Inc. and Wizards of the Coast.

He's currently working on a series of paintings and drawings for an upcoming art book, a series of self published illustrated prose works, and writing and directing independent films with close friend and studiomate, Kent Williams.

He drinks too much scotch and has become a big fan of Tom Waits.

ALSO AVAILABLE FROM GREG RUCKA AND BANTAM BOOKS...

A FISTFUL OF RAIN
Hardcover Edition
$23.95
ISBN 0-553-80135-X

"Rucka blends Spillaine's 'tough-guy' private eye with Chandler's noir insights and Hemingway's Spartan expression..." – Statesman Journal, Salem, Oregon

THE ATTICUS KODIAK NOVELS

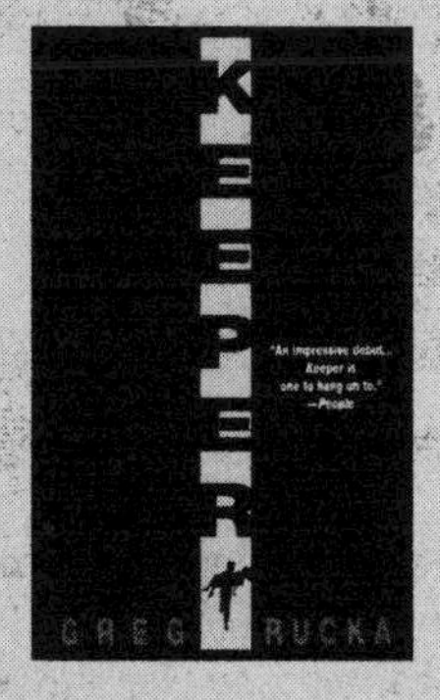

Keeper
$5.99 US
ISBN 0-553-57428-0

Finder
$5.99 US
ISBN 0-553-57429-9

Smoker
$5.99 US
ISBN 0-553-57829-4

Shooting At Midnight
$5.99 US
ISBN 0-553-57827-8

Critical Space
$6.99 US
ISBN 0-553-58179-1

AVAILABLE AT FINER BOOKSTORES EVERYWHERE.

Other books from Greg Rucka and Oni Press

"Greg Rucka is not a lesser writer. As an author, he thrives in political, moral and emotional complexity."

– *Warren Ellis, creator of* Transmetropolitan *and* Global Frequency

Queen & Country™ Vol. 1
Operation: Broken Ground
by Greg Rucka, Steve Rolston & Stan Sakai
128 pages • black-and-white interiors
$11.95 US • ISBN 1-929998-21-X

Queen & Country™ Vol. 2
Operation: Morningstar
by Greg Rucka, Brian Hurtt,
Bryan O'Malley, and Christine Norrie
88 pages • black-and-white interiors
$8.95 US • ISBN 1-929998-35-X

"Whiteout's *well researched, well written and expertly rendered. Don't buy it for those reasons, though. Buy it because Carrie Stetko's mouthy, freckled and cool...*"

– *Kelly Sue DeConnick, artbomb.net*

Queen & Country™ Vol. 3
Operation: Crystal Ball
by Greg Rucka & Leandro Fernandez
144 pages • black-and-white interiors
$14.95 US • ISBN 1-929998-49-X

Queen & Country™ Vol. 4
Operation: Blackwall
by Greg Rucka & J. Alexander
88 pages • black-and-white interiors
$9.95 US • ISBN 1-929998-68-6

For a comics store near you, call 1-888-COMIC-BOOK or visit www.the-master-list.com.

For more information on more Oni Press books go to: www.onipress.com

Queen & Country™ Vol. 5
Operation: Storm Front
by Greg Rucka &
Carla Speed McNeil
152 pages • black-and-white interiors
$14.95 US • ISBN 1-929998-84-8

Queen & Country™ Vol. 6
Operation: Dandelion
by Greg Rucka & Mike Hawthorne
120 pages • black-and-white interiors
$11.95 US • 1-929998-99-0

Whiteout™
by Greg Rucka & Steve Lieber
128 pages • black-and-white interiors
$11.95 US • ISBN 0-9667127-1-4

Whiteout: Melt™
by Greg Rucka & Steve Lieber
128 pages • black-and-white interiors
$11.95 US • ISBN 1-929998-03-1

Queen & Country™
Declassified Vol. 1
by Greg Rucka & Brian Hurtt
96 pages • black-and-white interiors
$8.95 US • ISBN 1-929998-58-9